12/13

W9-BRR-403

Dear Parents and Educators,

Welcome to Penguin Young Readers! As parents and educators, you know that each child develops at his or her own pace—in terms of speech, critical thinking, and, of course, reading. Penguin Young Readers recognizes this fact. As a result, each Penguin Young Readers book is assigned a traditional easy-to-read level (1–4) as well as a Guided Reading Level (A–P). Both of these systems will help you choose the right book for your child. Please refer to the back of each book for specific leveling information. Penguin Young Readers features esteemed authors and illustrators, stories about favorite characters, fascinating nonfiction, and more!

## Peter Rabbit™
## I Am Lily

LEVEL **2**

GUIDED READING LEVEL **E**

This book is perfect for a **Progressing Reader** who:
• can figure out unknown words by using picture and context clues;
• can recognize beginning, middle, and ending sounds;
• can make and confirm predictions about what will happen in the text; and
• can distinguish between fiction and nonfiction.

Here are some **activities** you can do during and after reading this book:
• Character Traits: In this story, Lily wants to become friends with Peter and Benjamin. Write down some words that describe Lily. Then write a list of words that describe Peter and Benjamin. Do you think they will be good friends? Why?
• Make Connections: Lily is new in town. Discuss a time when you were someplace new and had to make new friends. How did you feel? How did you make friends?

Remember, sharing the love of reading with a child is the best gift you can give!

—Bonnie Bader, EdM
  Penguin Young Readers program

*Penguin Young Readers are leveled by independent reviewers applying the standards developed by Irene Fountas and Gay Su Pinnell in *Matching Books to Readers: Using Leveled Books in Guided Reading*, Heinemann, 1999.

Penguin Young Readers
Published by the Penguin Group
Penguin Group (USA) Inc., 375 Hudson Street, New York, New York 10014, USA

USA | Canada | UK | Ireland | Australia | New Zealand | India | South Africa | China
Penguin Books Ltd, Registered Offices: 80 Strand, London WC2R 0RL, England

For more information about the Penguin Group visit penguin.com

All rights reserved. No part of this book may be reproduced, scanned, or distributed in any printed or
electronic form without permission. Please do not participate in or encourage piracy of copyrighted
materials in violation of the author's rights. Purchase only authorized editions.

*Peter Rabbit* television series imagery © Frederick Warne & Co. Ltd & Silvergate PPL Ltd, 2013.
Text, layout, and design © Frederick Warne & Co. Ltd, 2013.

The *Peter Rabbit* television series is based on the works of Beatrix Potter.
"Peter Rabbit" and "Beatrix Potter" are trademarks of Frederick Warne & Co.
Frederick Warne & Co. is the owner of all rights, copyrights, and trademarks in the
Beatrix Potter character names and illustrations.

Published by Penguin Young Readers, an imprint of Penguin Group (USA) Inc.,
345 Hudson Street, New York, New York 10014. Manufactured in China.

*Library of Congress Cataloging-in-Publication Data is available.*

ISBN 978-0-7232-8074-3 (pbk)     10 9 8 7 6 5 4 3 2
ISBN 978-0-7232-8083-5 (hc)      10 9 8 7 6 5 4 3 2 1

# Peter Rabbit™

# I Am Lily

Penguin Young Readers
An Imprint of Penguin Group (USA) Inc.

I am Lily.

Lily Bobtail.

I just moved here.

My only friend is Florence.

She is my pet ladybug.

I want to become friends with

Peter and Benjamin.

Peter is brave.

Benjamin is funny.

I know I will like them.

But they are not so sure
about me.

They do not know that

I am brave.

And smart.

I go with Peter and Benjamin

to the garden.

Look at all the things to eat.

# Berries!

Oh no!

There is a cat.

# Run!

Oh no!

Benjamin is stuck.

I help Peter pull Benjamin out.

We must get out of the garden.

We run past the scarecrow.

But I am not scared.

We go to our treehouse.

The treehouse is our secret place.

25

We make plans inside

our treehouse.

Then we go outside.

I am good at finding things
that are lost.

Now Peter and Benjamin

know who I am.

I am brave.

And smart.

And a lot of fun.

But most of all,

I am a great friend!